An Entitlement Upshot

ROSHANE LEWIS

Copyright © 2022 Roshane Lewis

An Entitlement Upshot

All Right Reserved. No part of this publication may be reproduced, stored in a retrieval system, or transmitted in any form or by any means, electronic or otherwise, without the prior written permission of the author.

This is a work of fiction. Characters and locations in this novel are the products of the author's imagination or, if real, used fictitiously with no intent to describe their actual conduct.

Communique ResourceHub edited and published this edition info@udunmaikoro.com

Cover & InDesign by SeedWorks Cynosure

seedworkscynosure@gmail.com

Table of Content

Dear Reader,

I am grateful for your purchase of this book. An Entitlement Upshot is a series that you will enjoy reading. Also, you will experience different views while you read on, feel free to share them. Marvina is a single mom that loves her children and would also make the best decisions for them. What happened when she had enough of her oldest child's substandard behaviors? This book is an introduction of what is to come. Stay tuned and connected.

Yours truly,

Roshane Lewis;

Creator of An Entitlement Upshot

Prologue

"Travis, we got five million from the robberies. This world is ours for the taking," said Guts, Travis's right-hand man. "It was like taking candy from a baby," he continued. Guts will boast after every mission he completed with the goons. Though he knows Travis hates the bragging, Guts could not contain himself. Pissing off the boss was just unavoidable. Let us look at where it all began; how Travis became the leader of the most powerful gang on the Island of Jamaica.

Chapter one

Santania, the Instigator!

"I am so tired of this nonsense!" Marvina emphasizes to her best friend, Santania. "What is it this time?" She asked, rolling her eyes in exasperation.

Santania is tired of Marvina's frequent complaints about the same situations without taking any action.

"Travis still refuses to show me respect in my house that I am paying the bills and not a help from his feckless dad,"

Marvina complained. "So, what happened this time?" Santania instigated. "Travis left his baby sister alone after I instructed him to babysit her until I got back from work. He turned his phone off too," Marvina assumed.

"I know he is out there doing some unscrupulous things with those street boys. I should have left him in Jamaica with his sorry, good for nothing dad," Marvina murmured. She would never give up an opportunity to speak negatively about Ryan, Travis's dad, which shows that she was not quite over him.

"Hey, hold up now. Ryan is far from sorry. My brother is doing well in his tire business." Santania claimed. Ryan was Santania's favorite out of all her siblings. Even with his gambling addiction, she would not ignore anyone talking poorly about him.

"Whatever! I regret that you introduced him to me," Marvina replied in despair. "Hey, I have known you since High School, and when have I not been on your side?"

Santania asked vividly. Marvina rolled her eyes at her without a reply." I'm just saying, forget about his feckless father and move on. Moreover, I already told you what to do with Travis," Santania declared.

"So let me get this straight. You want me to take my 13-year-old son back to Jamaica and leave him with his grandparents?" Marvina asked. "Yes! Five years like Manifest," Santania suggested. "If you cannot leave him with his grandparents, leave him with his dad or uncle. You have options." She added.

In the middle of the conversation, the door swung wide open. Travis walked inside the house abruptly from the kitchen entrance. He then proceeded upstairs to his bedroom, passing his mom and aunt as if they were invisible, slamming the door behind him. Once again, he displayed more of his apathetic behavior.

"Trust me; Jamaica will straighten him out," said Santania, who insisted on convincing Marvina. She welcomed the consultation, Santania was not fond of Travis and would make a quick referral against him.

After the separation from Ryan, Marvina thought she could raise Travis all by herself with no family members interfering. Now, she is open to suggestions from Travis's aunt. At first, Marvina made it clear that she did not want anyone schooling her kids. This happened during an argument at Marvina's house, after Santania spoke sternly to Travis because he jumped from one couch to the next. Marvina convinced herself that migrating from Jamaica with Travis was the best decision economically, hoping to improve the standard of living, growing up in America, the land of opportunities. She ignored other factors that were essential and could affect his behavior like; not having a father figure in his life. Also, he always heard his mom talk negatively about his dad. Which caused Travis to lose respect for Ryan, instead of being open to his guidance.

The attitudes Travis saw his friends had towards their parents also played a huge part in his behavior. His frequent visits to their homes influenced him. Travis adapted to his friend's lifestyle, soaking up every bit like a sponge, while Marvina was busy working extra hours as a single parent to prevent the collapse of her home. Unfortunately, she noticed his deviation when it was beyond her control; hopefully, the same thing won't happen to her daughter Trisha.

A few months had passed, and Travis continued with his ill-mannered and uncivilized conduct. He would constantly miss the bus, skip school, get suspended for fighting, talk back to his mom, get home late, locked inside his room all day, and play video games without a bath or doing his chores.

Marvina was exhausted. She came to the conclusion that waiting for him to change was pointless. Finally, she decided that Travis needed to face some consequences of his actions. Maybe, the Santania method could be the ideal way, and summer the optimum timing.

"Travis, they released Uncle Floyd from jail, and he will stay with you for a week," Marvina declared.
"What do you mean, stay with me, and where will you be?" Travis asked. "Well, your sister and I will travel to Jamaica, unless you want to come with us," she suggested. Travis quickly jumped at the opportunity. "I sure do. I do not want to stay here with your crazy brother." Travis complained.

"Well, consider this an early 14th birthday present," Marvina announced. "Along with the Xbox, iPhone, and the new pair of Jordans?" Travis asked. Inconsiderately, Travis had the mindset of getting whatever he desires, always having the highest expectations and no regards for his mom's struggles. Travis being unsympathetic enough to specify that this is part of his entitlement as a child.

Marvina wanted to weigh the intensity of disgust towards Travis but dug deeper. It took everything in her not to lash out at him about the video games and shoes. Clearly, he did not deserve it. However, Marvina managed to maintain a smile on her face, which was nothing but a deceitful act.

Chapter two

The Resort

The plane landed in Montego Bay, Jamaica, on August 1st, two weeks before Travis's 14th birthday. He was excited his mom had no problems with him bringing his video games, IPad, and laptop. Previously, she would've had issues if he packed an excess suitcase, but this time she told him to bring everything he would need.

Marvina planned to stay at an all-inclusive beachfront resort in Montego Bay for the first five days to enjoy this brief interval of respite. She had no plan to boycott her vacation. Albeit, she had ulterior motives.

After checking in at the front desk, they received the keys for the two rooms. Travis was in a separate room next to the luxurious one occupied by his mom and younger sister, Trisha. The room had a Jacuzzi at the window. Marvina's favorite was the idyllic view from the balcony to the sands and the beautiful blue waves. Marvina quickly got dressed in her black, green, and gold two-piece bathing suit, anxious to show off her new body after the Brazilian Butt Lift surgery.

After being in front of the mirror gazing, swirling, and posing repeatedly, Marvina wrapped her tiny waist with her favorite black, green, and gold Marley towel. That was as far as her modesty goes until her feet touch the sands. In addition, with her frequent visits to the bar for the complimentary cocktails, she went to bed every night with a peaceful and tranquil mind.

Travis and Trisha were mostly delighted with the food. Having breakfast, lunch, and dinner at their service. The cake and ice cream were captivating to them being voracious eaters; they wished it never had to come to an end.
"Travis, I want to go down to the beach where mom is. Could you take me?" Trisha asked in her frail voice.

Travis ignored her. Though he was lenient and protective towards his baby sister, he never liked to be disturbed while playing video games online with his friends. "Travis, Travis, Travis!!" She nagged again and again. "Ok! Travis hissed with irritation; He threw his controller on the bed, turned the TV off, and blamed her after a sorry loss.

Together, they made their way to the elevator which took them to the first floor where the food and beverages were.

Travis stopped on the way to get a bowl of Rum Raisin ice cream, eager to get a taste after hearing his mom endorse it over the years. Finally Travis and his sister made it to the beach. Their mom was lying on her towel next to her friend and her daughter.

"These are my kids, Travis and Trisha, and this is Emily and her daughter, Woo." Marvina introduced everyone frankly. Travis said hi to Emily in the most respectful way he could while he stuttered before saying hi to her daughter. Obviously, Travis was mesmerized by the beautiful Woo.

After meeting Woo, Travis no longer wanted to stick to his regular routine of eating and playing video games. He instantly became a huge fan of the beach. The ladies and their kids were sitting at the beach enjoying the tidal up to the sand before Travis grabbed the beach ball and threw it to his sister, playing at the edge of the water. Travis hoped that Woo would eventually join, but she gave only a vacant stare or smirk. She was not interested in playing with any ten year old. Woo was oblivious to the environment; her phone had most of her attention.

That was the final day at the resort. It was the longest Travis had been out of his room. He was unaware of his mom having friends there and was definitely sorry he had less time to get acquainted with Woo. After all, she was the most beautiful girl he had ever laid his eyes on.

After they left the beach and were on their way back to the room, Marvina stated, "Hurry up, Travis! Uncle Richie doesn't like waiting, even though he is late. I bet he will still be in a no-nonsense mood when he gets here." Marvina knew Uncle Richie as one who never liked to wait on anyone, but you can always count on him to show up late.

The phone rang, it was Santania. "Hey girl, what's up?" She asked. "Just trying to hurry before Uncle Richie gets here," Marvina replied. "As you know, I have to be on Travis's tail to ensure he leaves nothing in his room," she added. "Hold up, do not tell me you gave Travis a whole room by himself?" Santania questioned. "Well, you know how he is. Travis made it clear that he didn't want to stay with us," Marvina explained.

"You see! This is exactly the kind of crap why he feels so entitled," Santania argued. She blames Marvina for Travis's behavior. "How many days?" She queries. "Five days," Marvina revealed. "Five days!" "For Travis in a room all by himself, at a resort? "His last name must be Scott!" Again, Santania instigates like she normally would. "Girl, bye! I made it to work. I will call you back on my lunch break," she stated.

Uncle Richie finally arrived at the resort in a black minivan hurrying everyone even though he was over forty-five minutes late.

"Marvina, I am here at the front desk. I do not see you walking towards me yet," Uncle Richie grumbled on the phone. Marvina and Trisha made their way to the van hauling their suitcases, Travis leading the way. He said 'hey' to Uncle Richie, quickly put his bag in, and took a seat at the back of the van.

"Boy, if you don't get your Rosa Parks self out of the van and help your mom and your sister with their suitcases!" Uncle Richie strongly suggested. Travis immediately went and put the suitcases inside the trunk; he forcefully shoved the bags inside about four times. "That is good now," Uncle Richie declared. Travis continued to shove the suitcases indicating that he was mad. "I said, that was good!" Uncle Richie repeated himself before slamming the van's door shut with Travis's fingers barely escaping the wrath.

Chapter three

Travis Called 119

Marvina received a call from Travis only a couple of weeks later after leaving him in Jamaica with his dad. That was the hardest thing she had to do in her lifetime. Of course, she had a change of heart at the end, but every time Marvina crumbled, Santania never failed to remind her of the importance, guiding her to ignore Travis's ranting.

"Mom, you have to get me out of this place. Dad is crazy," Travis complained. "He gets mad for the simplest things. I told him that I finished Junior High School and will not be going back. He got mad," Travis explained. "Travis, did you use the 'F' word?" Marvina asked. "It doesn't matter if I did; he is crazy!" Travis emphasized, hoping that his mom would be remorseful about leaving him in Jamaica.

"Travis, didn't I inform you that in Jamaica, Junior High Schools go up to the 9th grade? It doesn't end in the 8th grade like here in America," Marvina clarified. Santania urged Marvina to put the phone on speaker, so that she could have a laugh at Travis and she insisted until Marvina complied.

"Anyway, what did he do to you this time?" Marvina asked, her voice sounding like she was already in disbelief.

Once again, before Travis could finish his statement, Marvina showed refusal to accept the story about his dad. She found out that Travis was untruthful in his three previous complaints. Hence, she did not believe anything from Travis's lying tongue.

"He held the machete in his left hand and punched me seven times with his right," Travis exaggerated, hoping that Marvina would empathize with him. "Ryan would never do such a thing," Marvina replied, even though she was quick to speak negatively of Travis's dad, she never believed a word that was coming out of her son's mouth. "Tell him to call the police," Santania whispered, doing what she does best, being an instigator.

Marvina quickly put the phone on mute; before replying to Santania, she hoped Travis wouldn't notice."No, he cannot do that," Marvina mentioned. "What did he do the last time you hit him while he was here? He called the police, right?" Santania asked. Marvina shook her head in affirmative response to the question. "Call 119," Marvina told Travis. "What's that number for?" Travis asked. "It is the emergency number there in Jamaica, the police will resolve it," said Marvina.

"Mom, just get me out of here, please," he begged. "Ok, I'll ask Uncle Richie if you can stay with him," Marvina mocked, knowing that Uncle Richie acted wrathfully at the hotel in Montego Bay. "No, I am good," Travis replied as he disrespectfully hung the phone up.
The police arrived at Ryan's house about two hours after Travis made the phone call to the police station.

Upon arrival, they could see residents on their phones making calls. It was clear that they were all trying to alert the area don, who at that time was a man named Roger Harris with the nickname Gunhand.

Each community in the ghetto had a gang leader referred to as the don, who was in charge.

The don and his goons worked like a local justice organization protecting the community from robberies, rapes or any sort of violence. Anyone who breaches the community laws would receive discipline as the don best sees fit. A call for the cops to enter the community violates this law. The residents complied with the mindset that this was substantially built because the police force did not prove to be trustworthy.

After the cops made their way to the destination, Travis informed them about Ryan's abusive actions towards him, especially punching him repeatedly.

"So, you called us here to waste our time because your dad punched you?" Asked Corporal Sherine Johnson. "Yes, ten times," Travis responded, this time he went for a higher number than what he mentioned to Marvina. He hoped that it would be more effective. "I do not care if it was a thousand times." Corporal Johnson mentioned. "You had to do something to deserve it." She stated.

"Officers, he needed to be disciplined. He was disrespectful to his mom, and he thought he could do the same to me." Ryan explained himself to the cops.

Corporal Sherine Johnson then turned to Travis and asked, "You think this is America?" Then, she added, "you have a next guess coming." Using one of Jamaica's favorite terms, which means, there will be an unpleasant surprise.

Chapter four

Woo to the Rescue

About 30 minutes after the police left, two of the don's goons approached Ryan. "The general needs to see you," said Elusive, who was second in command to the don. "Bring Tireman too," he added. The don lived at the end of the lane, about seven blocks away from Ryan's house.

The four made their way to the don's house, with Ryan and Travis leading the way, followed by Elusive and Guts, the don's most vicious cronies.

Travis was reluctant the entire journey until he arrived in the don's backyard where he witnessed a brutal beating on one of his neighbors by some of the don's cronies. They used batons to beat Travis's neighbor while the others stood around, watching with handguns and rifles.

"Do you have a problem with the system?" Gunhand asked Travis calmly. "No, he was uninformed," Travis's dad responded before Travis said anything slick that would cost him a leg. Besides, Ryan knew how vicious Gunhand could be even in his calmest state, especially with his goons there.

"Well, one of his hands will need plaster after this visit," Gunhand spoke frankly. Travis was about to lose his composure. Ryan kept him calm knowing that the situation could easily escalate and cause Travis to lose his life instead. "He broke the most important rule of the community, so in return, I have to break something." Gunhand declared calmly again like it was just another walk in the park.

"What if I can pay for my hand?" Travis inquires. "What do you mean exactly?" Gunhand asked. Travis was quite intelligent for his age; he was a quick thinker and a straight-A student. Even with his misbehaving, Travis's teachers could not deny his brilliance. His peers referred to him as a genius.

"What if I could give you some money by the end of this month?" Travis clarified.

Gunhand hesitated for a while. He was not about to take Travis's offer. He was more concerned about his reputation and how it would appear as a sign of weakness if he let that sort of action go unpunished.

Travis thought he had the brilliance to circumvent any situation that allowed him to converse amicably; this was the case where his luck would surely run out.

Suddenly, the back door of the don's house swung wide open. A girl about Travis's age rushed outside. "Daddy, daddy my school fees and books are still unpaid for; don't forget about the school trip, plus you promised to book my ticket so that I can visit mom," the girl said with an angelic voice.

"Woo, not now! Woo, don't you see I am in the middle of something? Get back inside," Gunhand demanded.

Woo took her time walking back inside the house, hoping it would give her dad enough time to process all those expenses, and realize that taking the money would not be such a terrible idea. Even though Woo cared little about the money, she didn't want Travis to get hurt.

"One week, $2,000," Gunhand demanded. "Since when did you speak US currencies?" Ryan asked, finally getting some courage after being scared the entire time. "Since I am dealing with an American," Gunhand replied vividly.

Travis and Ryan left Gunhand's house and were on their way back to their home when Ryan asked Travis, "Where are we going to get that amount of money from, son? "Mommy, of course; I cannot depend on you and your tire shop," Travis responded insolently. "Damn right," Ryan replied.

"Plus, I know it is a few weeks from crumbling with all your debts," Travis continued, asking for another round of punches like he had earlier that day.

Anyway, since I need some money and so do you, I have the perfect plan that might work for both of us," Travis mentioned. "And what might that be?" Ryan asked. "I'll tell mom we need $5,000, give Gunhand his $2,000, and we will split the rest 50/50," Travis suggested, showing his dad how cruel and rogue he can be.

At first, Ryan scoffed at the idea. He could not believe what he heard and how nonchalant Travis was. As desperate as Ryan was, he didn't know if he should be proud or disappointed, but one thing was for sure, Ryan wasn't one to turn down money. "You think Marvina will send that much money?" Ryan asked his son. "Well, as tough as mommy pretends to be with Santania in her ears, I know she would book the next flight if she saw me in plaster," Travis declared. "I just need you to play your part well when it comes," he projected.

"Hold on! I thought you wanted to leave?" His dad asked. "I realize it is not so bad after all. I might do even better here," he claimed. Ryan could not figure out why Travis had a sudden change of heart, but it did not matter. All he needed was the money so he could pay the bank for them not to seize his assets. "Since I will tell a lie, and I have never told any in my lifetime, we will split the remaining seventy to me, thirty to you," Ryan suggested. Ryan's gambling habits gave him constant desperation for money, so Travis wasn't surprised by his greed.

Chapter five

Woo; the Predominant Soul.

"I had to attend church just to see you," Travis whispered while sitting on a bench inside the Pentecostal Church. The church was the only one in the community and was located at the front next to the main street; Travis could easily see Woo entering early. "Wrong reason to visit Church," Woo replied with a straight face, pretending as if she wasn't delighted to see him.

Church continued for another hour, but Woo was an usher and the lead singer of the Choir. They preoccupied her with the Church festivities; Travis barely got a word in. He could only stare and smile while waiting out the long four hours service.

Church finally ended. Woo immediately exited the door and tried hard to get out of Travis's sight.

Travis knew that Woo was trying to protect him by staying away. It did not scare him, even though he knew her family history and had experienced it firsthand.

Travis rushed out after Woo, stepping in front of her in the middle of the Church yard before she exited the main gate.

Woo looked directly at Travis and spoke strenuously. "Let me guess; you are here to show your gratitude? I do not need your thanks. I did what was necessary because your mom and my mom are friends," Woo stated clearly before turning her back towards him and was about to walk away.

Travis stepped in front of her again, showing perseverance. "That could be the case, or maybe I just like you," Travis claimed. "You like me! Or you like trouble?" Woo asked. Travis was about to answer, but before he could even get his words out, Woo added, "either way, it still spells trouble," she declared.

However she was flattered. "Remind me of your name again?" Woo asked. "Travis," he quickly replied. "No, not that one. The name I heard everyone calling you that is the one I like," Woo claimed. "You like the name Tireman? Can this conversation get any weirder? Travis asked. "Well, that way, I know you are good for something and neither a scammer nor a drug dealer; just in case I have to introduce you someday," she stated.

"You cannot bring me home to your dad, even if I was the Pastor. Meanwhile, a scammer or a drug dealer might be the ideal son-in-law for him. You might win a medal." Travis jeered. "He got jokes, funny American. Maybe you deserve a broken hand after all," she spoke harshly before walking away.

Travis did not stop her again; he had little to say. Nevertheless, Woo had impressed him without even trying. That was the first time Travis had ever come across a girl his age that was way more outspoken than he was.

Woo was only a year older than Travis. She was already in high school as a freshman in the ninth grade, but with Travis's height and muscular features, he presented himself to be one year older.

In the ghetto, Woo was that female hated by many of her peers because of her high integrity and introverted nature which resulted in isolation. But her peers kept the hate they felt towards her quiet because of her dad's status. Woo showed her face mostly at church, school, or the annual spelling bee competition hosted every year by her dad. Woo was the winner every time; the loathe grew stronger.

Woo was remarkable. Her dad had never been a cheerful person. Still, Woo's grades and achievements would easily make him endure feelings of euphoria. She was motivated by her own enthusiasm, concerned with her own thoughts and commitments to her religious beliefs. Of the family, church, school, and community Woo was the predominant soul.

Even though she grew up in a violent home and violent community, Woo did not emulate her parents' lifestyles. She would never allow her environment to define her. Woo would still share her views that differed totally from her father's. She did not believe in the jungle justice, but Woo preferred her dad having the last say than someone else as young, dodgy, and heartless as Elusive. Elusive was second in command. If her dad leaves, he would wear the title of the don.

Woo hoped her dad would continue to make the best decisions for the community based on his expertise. Elusive would turn things upside down. He is not one to reckon with. Woo also pressed her father about giving back to the community. She constantly reminded him of the respect they gave him so that he would not make any mistakes that could turn into fear. "People will not protect you if you inflict fear. They see it as a threat, and the first instinct towards any threat is to eradicate," those were Woo's direct words.

Chapter six

Elusive, the Unfortunate

Elusive was only 19 when he became the most wanted on the island. He was always on the run from police officers and moved quite often. They associated him with about 25 murders in six months, his name also in all the fourteen Parishes of Jamaica.

The police attempted to corner Elusive, but each encounter started with a shootout and Elusive disappearing in the end. Just like the definition of his name, he was as slippery as an eel.

Sheldon Foster, known as Elusive, was born in Spanish Town, St Catherine, but raised by his grandparents in St Elizabeth after becoming an orphan at ten years old. Elusive's dad was a contractor, and his mom was a teacher. His parents first met at a High School where his mom worked for over 15 years.

Elusive's dad, Gilbert, had the skills to build a house from scratch with just a glance at the blueprint. He was from St Elizabeth, but he migrated to Spanish Town, where he lived with Kira after the birth of their son, Elusive. Gilbert built most of the biggest houses on Walks Road, including the lovely three-bedroom house he built for his wife, Kira. The plan was to have another child like she always wanted, to complete the family of four.

Gilbert and Kira had almost the perfect family life, raising their son in the church where Kira was a missionary and Gilbert was the Bishop. About seven months after Gilbert became a member of the church, he volunteered to develop the entire structure. Over a period of time Gilbert carried out some carpentry, tiling, painting, electrical and masonry works, making the building sturdier. With more comfortable chairs there were fewer complaints about back pains. Gilbert was doing what he loved, and he enjoyed it even more because he was doing it for God.

One day, Gilbert was approached by Casper, the most wanted fugitive in the area in the late 90s.

"I want you to build a one-bedroom house for me," Casper strongly suggested. He assumed that Gilbert already feared his appearance like the other residents in the community would.

"Casper, you think that is a good idea? You do not think you should go cool out elsewhere?" Gilbert asked, hoping that

Casper would consider his suggestion and leave the community so that it could be a safer place for him and his family.

"No, Gilbert. It's not for me, but for my mother. I know my time is near, and I want to leave her with something before then," Casper stated. "Besides, I know you guys attend the same church. You might do it for free," he added.

"That's not how it works, plus she just got baptized only four days ago," Gilbert declared, thinking that they were trying to make a fool out of him. "Why does it matter?" Casper asked "She was putting money in the offering plate long before baptism," He spoke threateningly. Gilbert did not reply. He perceived an argument could spring up, and he wanted to make sure that was avoided.

"Let me know how much it will cost. I will give you half before the work starts and the other half whenever you finish. That is the least you can do for a member," Casper claimed.

At the end of the conversation, Gilbert went home and shared his encounter with his wife, Kira. "You are not working for Casper!" Kira stated. "The only one room he will get is a coffin," she added. Though Kira was a female she proved to be the most unyielding of the two. "Do not say that. We know he is evil, but he is still Mrs. Carleen's son," Gilbert declared. He was always lenient and quick to help others in their most troubled times.

Gilbert had completed the one-bedroom house for Casper by the first three months of the deposit. He still waited on the last payment, even though six more months had passed. It had been a whole nine months since the beginning of their contract.

"I told you not to do any work for Casper," Kira said to Gilbert over the phone. She was always quick to say I told you so. "I'm going over there now to tell him and the backslider a piece of my mind. I haven't seen Mrs Carleen in church for a whole six months!" She brawled with the feeling that they had deceived her husband once more. She wasn't about to leave it in God's hands this time.

"Kira, Kira!" Gilbert called. Once he realized the call had ended, he hurried to Casper's house. He hoped to get there before his wife. Knowing the type of person they were dealing with, Gilbert was cautious, but not Kira.

As soon as Gilbert and Kira made it over to Casper's house, they found themselves in the middle of a shootout between the police and Casper. With the head of the operation Senior Superintendent of Police Aaron Roberts who led the most vicious police unit on the island. SSP Aaron Roberts promoted the concept of shooting first and then asked questions later.

With Casper pinned down having no escape route, and no help from his goons who had no genuine respect for him but only fear for his cruelty. The gun battle lasted about thirty minutes, afterwards the news reported that the police had killed Casper, Gilbert, and Kira who were a part of a deadly gang.

The residents were devastated about the loss of Gilbert and Kira but again justice was never served. Their death resulted in Elusive quickly moving from a child with everything he ever wanted to an orphan. As Elusive grew older, the unhappy memories receded in his mind.

Chapter seven

Spelling Bee Championship

"Son, have you heard about the Spelling Bee Competition?" Ryan asked Travis. "No, I'm not interested," Travis replied. "You could win 30,000 JMD easily, "Ryan suggested. Ryan had a keen interest anywhere money gets involved; it did not matter the amount. "Still not interested," Travis stressed. Ryan wouldn't take no for an answer. He wanted the money to support his gambling habits, as usual.

"You know that would make your mom extremely proud if you win the competition," Ryan continued to press the issue. "Have you seen my grades? I've been making my mother proud! I am not in that mind space to enter a competition," Travis stated. "So, you're just going to let Woo walk away with the prize?" Ryan asked, deliberately mentioning Woo, knowing that would catch Travis's attention.

Travis pretended that his father mentioning Woo didn't capture his interest, so he left the house to open up the tire shop for the day.

At the shop, Travis had a deep contemplation about entering the Spelling Bee Competition. He thought maybe this would be an opportunity to get close to Woo and even impress her. Travis already knew that his dad would be happy to give him the 500 JMD for the entry fee because he was confident about Travis winning. However, Travis also had his own money stashed away.

Later that day, Travis was outside the tire shop when he heard two gunshots fired. At first, Travis could not tell what direction it was coming from. Suddenly, he saw Elusive jumped over the wall of another business place on the right side of the tire shop. Then, he ran past him.

Outside the tire shop, there were three stacks of tires for advertisement. Travis pushed over the stack of tires into the narrow roadway before a police vehicle came around the corner with excessive speed. With no way around the tires, the driver had no choice but to stop.

There weren't any sirens. But, based on the stories Travis heard, he knew there was no civilian powerful enough to make Elusive run. So Travis assumed it was the police before the car even came around the corner.

After the driver stepped out of the vehicle, Travis noticed it was Corporal Sherine Johnson, stamping her feet and shaking her head, showing just how furious she was. She swore to kill Elusive from the day he executed the only person in the community that would rat him out.

Corporal Johnson saw Travis looking out at her through the window of the tire shop. She walked over to him and said, "after years of attempts, you prevented one of the most wanted criminals from being captured today." If you think that was an achievement, then I will be looking forward to chasing you down in the streets one day and trust me, you will not be that lucky," she swore. The loathe that she felt for Elusive now extended to Travis. She was zealous in her pursuit of criminal activities.

"Tireman saved Elusive's life!" Those were the words that traveled quickly around the community. In the evening, Elusive visited Travis at the tire shop with Guts, his protégé. "You saved my life today. You are pretty brave for your age. Where did you get that bravery from?" Elusive asked Travis. "I might be young, but I have been in these streets," Travis answered boastfully.

"That I understand. I've been here early myself," Elusive mentioned. "Well, I guess I owe you one. Anything you need, let me know. If anyone messes with you, let me know," he declared. "Well, no one messed with me, but there is something you could do for both of us," Travis stated. Elusive's mind was already full of questions about Travis, his curiosity might finally be satisfied. "Can we speak privately?" Travis asked. Elusive did not hesitate. He gave Guts the signal to step outside while he spoke with Travis.

"Gunhand, you need to get rid of him. You should be the Don," Travis strongly suggested. "Careful! I said that I owe you one, but do not get it over your head," Elusive replied, pretending that he had never thought of it before. "I didn't suggest killing him, but a change in leadership would not be such a bad idea," Travis clarified. "The community will never accept me as their leader, Gunhand takes care of them, plus they respect him," Elusive explained.

"Yes, but they fear you," Travis reveals. "What about taking care of you and the goons? I don't see him doing that very well," he added to convince Elusive with a plausible argument in his effort. "What do you mean?" Elusive questioned, hoping that Travis would have a good enough proposal that he could share with the goons and get them on his side to subdue Gunhand.

"The day he was about to break my hand, I offered him money, but he refused to take it. As soon as his daughter came out and gave him a rundown of his expenses, he agreed to only $2,000. Do you see where I'm going with this?" Travis asked. "No, not yet, but continue," Elusive replied.

"Well, it is clear he had no intention of sharing the money with you and the gang, so he had no reason to demand more," Travis stated. Once again, Elusive liked where the conversation was heading. "But if you want to continue following a leader that is desperate for money enough to bargain for $2,000, then so be it," Travis taunted.

"Are you saying there is another way?" Elusive asked. "Yes, get rid of Gunhand, take over leadership, and force all these business owners to pay extortion for their protection," Travis implied. He could be very persuasive and deceitful without any effort. Elusive was more than just impressed; he was delighted but decided not to display any act as if he agreed. Maybe, Travis is worth more than Guts, his protégé, he thought.

"What If they refuse?" Elusive asked Travis. "Then you will do what Elusive does best," Travis mentioned. Travis had the habit of telling people what they like to hear. It was part of his strategy to get closer so that he could eventually control or influence their behaviors.

Elusive already wanted to take over. It excites him that Travis had given a reasonable argument to share with the goons. That way he wouldn't jeopardize his loyalty, which would have indicated that he wasn't suitable for leadership.

"What is in it for you?" Elusive asked, not that he really cared; he was just curious.

"Whenever you get that weed stash from St. Elizabeth, start me off with a pound," Travis requested. He didn't want Gunhand dead; he just wanted someone he could probably control in the position. Travis stood no chance with Woo if Gunhand continued to have that much power. So, he capitalized on the opportunity to start a friendship with Elusive, who was vulnerable at the time after a near-death experience.

However Travis wasn't really interested in selling weed he was only giving Elusive more reasons to join forces with him, if he intended to take over Elusive's friendship was essential or at least for the moment.

Chapter eight

Tryouts

Two years had passed, and Travis was now 16 years old. He still wasn't successful with his intention of pursuing Woo, nor was Elusive successful in eliminating Gunhand. However, Elusive started Travis off with some weed as he requested. His name quickly diverted from Tireman to weed man. The weed business blossomed, and so did Travis and Elusive's friendship, with Travis having the intention of taking over the community by himself one day.

"Now that you both go to the same high school, seeing her shouldn't be a problem, right?" Elusive asked Travis. While hanging out at the tire shop, he eventually learned of Travis's affections for Woo. "Hardly. You already know how she likes to isolate herself, and when she sees me, she pretends as if she didn't," replied Travis in despair. Travis was now in the 10th grade and Woo in the 11th grade.

"I guess you thought winning the Spelling Bee competition would've pulled her closer to you. Instead, it did the opposite. She was embarrassed, based on her being older than you. Besides, the other girls hate her for thinking that she's better than them, her defeat made them rejoice," Elusive explained. "No, she doesn't think like that," Travis quickly spoke on her behalf. "Maybe you need to change your style. You cannot just be a regular schoolboy; you need a title to your name," Elusive suggested.

"Weed man, ain't good enough?" Travis asked. "For the typical female, yes, but not for Woo," Elusive pointed out. "You need to make some music or try out a sports team," he suggested positively. "I could try Track and Field," Travis mentioned. No! Any other sport but Track and field," Elusive directed.

"I've seen you grow into a skillful football player, and you might have more luck in that direction," Elusive stated. "Why not Track and field?" Travis asked, sounding confident in his speed. "Track and field is an individual sport. If you are not the best at your event, you still will not get recognition. Besides, this is Jamaica. Everyone is fast," Elusive explained.

"In football, you only need to make the team, and you are good," he clarified. "Remember, it is called football, not soccer," he added. Travis had some problems adjusting to the name; football when he returned to Jamaica because he became more familiar with calling the sport soccer back in America. However Jamaicans never liked when their favorite sport is referred to as soccer.

"By the way, you need to wear some Clarks and closer pants. By now you should already figure out the Jamaican style," Elusive jeered. "I don't wear those skinny jeans," he declared, showing confidence in his dress code. "Travis leads he doesn't follow," he added. "Ok, where did leading get you so far?" Elusive asked, again he mocked Travis.

"So, is that why you are yet to kill Gunhand? Are you scared of leading?" Travis asked. "I am not scared of anything or anyone. By the way, when did we decide to kill him? I thought you said to get him out?" Elusive questions. "You would be more naïve than I thought if you expect to chase him off and he's just going to sit and accept his defeat,"

Travis stated. "Ok, let's see," he took his turn to jeer but Elusive wasn't one to Play with.

A few weeks later, Travis was walking to school, not having any school bus like when he was in America. At first, it was exhausting for him to get used to the Jamaican system. After two long years, he gradually did so, proving his resilience. In Travis's school bag, there were shorts, a pair of football shoes, and his favorite Messi t-shirt. After three weeks of showing extreme dedication to practicing some hardcore tricks, he was ready for tryouts.

Travis finally made it to the football field, eager to play after a long day in his class. He was a bit later than the other students; but not late enough to cause any cancellation of his tryouts. Travis made it to the field just as the other players were about to do some warm up exercises. He quickly introduced himself to the head coach, Mr. Neville. "First day, and you are late? Not a good look, Travis." Those were Neville's first direct words to him for the day and definitely won't be the last. "It will not happen again, coach," Travis claimed. "Trust me, I know," Neville replied. "Join the team. They will be doing fifteen laps around the field. I need five extra laps from you afterwards," the head coach, Mr. Neville, requested.

Travis rushed off to join the team, feeling nervous. He knew his tricks were sensational but needed a chance to prove it. "Travis!" Coach Neville shouted, then kicked a football powerfully in his direction. Travis turned around and controlled the ball with his chest, bouncing it off to his right thigh; before it touched the ground. He leaned slightly to his right and kicked it back powerfully to the Coach with his left foot.

Mr. Neville was the most accomplished coach in the league. He had his way of telling how good a player was by observation; from their first touch of the football. Indeed, Travis's first touch was impressive, the coach was able to tell that Travis was capable of using both left and right, which was rare. Mr. Neville still managed to maintain a straight face, not showing any gesture even though he was impressed.

Mr. Neville's experiences taught him how conceited the most talented players could be. So, his next move was to test Travis's discipline and fitness.

Travis jogged around the field as the coach instructed him. He struggled to keep up with the others. Before he could finish his fifteen laps, they had over-lapped him twice. Travis was exhausted. He didn't understand how they could run that fast; he seemed to be going in reverse. Suddenly, he remembered what Elusive had said to him about not joining Track and Field.

Travis finished all 20 laps and slowed down to join the others in their drill course. Then he heard the coach's voice, "one more lap, Travis," the coach demanded. Again, he tested Travis's patience. Mr. Neville had the loudest and most irritating voice you could ever imagine; the sound echoed in Travis's ears.

Travis was already weary; his legs ached, his face baked in the sun, and his shirt soaked with sweat. This last lap seemed even more strenuous than the 20 times he jogged around the field earlier. On his last lap he watched the other players skip through cones and took shots at the goal. Though tired, Travis eagerly wanted his turn.

By the time Travis finished the last lab, time for games. Mr. Neville split the team in two, one set of players in bibs and the other set without bibs. The game started, and Travis was all over the field chasing the ball, like a cat after a mouse. He urged his teammates for a pass so he could prove his skills.

After about fifteen minutes into the game, Mr. Neville already had enough of Travis being all over the field. He blew the whistle, stopped the game, and asked Travis. "What position do you play?" Travis had no clue what to say, so his reply was ambiguous. "I'm an all-rounder," "I see!" Neville mocked. Everyone laughed, unable to contain themselves. It was obvious that Travis knew how to play the game, but he didn't understand the positions involved.

"Let me ask you again; what position do you play?" Travis hesitated for a while and came up with the quickest answer, "Attacking left-back." They laughed again, even more brawling. The humiliation was more severe than before. Even the coaches thought it was hilarious.

"There is no such thing. You could be a defender, midfielder, or forward," Mr. Neville declared. "Hold on, I have the perfect position for you," he jeered. Mr. Neville walked with Travis towards the goal, then he ordered the goalkeeper. "Give Travis your gloves, and take his bib."

It devastated Travis; he wanted to opt out of the football game. Travis felt like they ostracized him from the group. He had never been that embarrassed a day in his life.

Chapter nine

Last Day of Tryouts

"Travis, first you wanted me to kill the don. Now, it is the coach. Who is next, your principal?" Elusive asked. "Man, I'm just asking you to do what Elusive does best." Travis proclaimed, hoping that Elusive's ego would deliver once more. "Didn't you say you owed me one?" He questioned. "Yes, and I gave you the weed. That is just about enough favor right there. Aren't there two more days of tryouts? There is still time for you to make the bench," Elusive mocked.

"Two more days, yes, but I do not think I can even make the bench," said Travis, already giving up after just one failed attempt. "I was too tired after the running. It felt like all my tricks were gone," Travis pondered. "That is because playing in the backyard is not equivalent to playing on the field. Your body is not used to such pressure," Elusive hints. "After a few laps, you easily become fatigued, unable to focus on your skills," Elusive explained.

Elusive's words were encouraging. It was the first time Travis heard him being passionate about anything. Usually, he would not have any care in the world. Elusive was a big football fan. With the dream of becoming a professional Footballer, the death of his parents led him on a totally different path.

With two more days of tryouts to go, Travis devised his unique strategy; He wouldn't go on the second day of tryouts, he skipped school to run as many miles as possible. Elusive taught him the positions of the game, but it was time to work on his endurance. It was not enough time for him to get as fit as the other players; but enough to execute his remarkable skills.

After a hard day of practicing at home and an early night's rest, Travis rejuvenated and was ready for the last day of tryouts. This time, he put in extra effort to reach the field before everyone. "Travis, I assumed you quit," said Neville, looking quite surprised, along with the other players and the rest of the coaching staff.

It was time to start their routine. While jogging around the field, Travis could barely keep up, but at least they did not overlap him this time. After the jogging, it was Travis's favorite, the shooting drill. He insisted on making an impact after he missed out the last time.

The coaches had thirty cones set up on the left side of the field, from the half-line down to the eighteen-yard box, and the same on the right side.

Each player would dribble as quickly as possible through the cones to score after passing the last cone, then join the line on the opposite side. The player needs to do the same with the opposite foot. The best goalkeeper on the team was at the goal line. It was an arduous task.

For Travis, the information given by the coach was easy assimilation. He scored every time with both feet. Travis was excited because scoring was his specialty. The only player that came close to Travis's goal-scoring tally was their main striker, Mikey. He was also the captain of the team. Mikey had the speed of light and swift, though he could not score with both feet like Travis.

It was finally time to play a game after the coach wrapped up the drills sessions. "What position do you play, Travis?"

Mr. Neville asked while everyone turned around, anticipating Travis's reply with his previous answer in mind. "I'm a forward," Travis stated sharply.

Mr. Neville placed Travis and Mikey on the opposite teams to see who would be the better striker. Again Travis's team wore bibs.

Mr. Neville knew that most players that show exceptional execution in drills do not give the same result during the pressure of the game. He wanted to see if Travis could progress and evolve with the team, not only individually.

The game finished four to three, with Mikey scoring four goals and Travis three goals. Travis was exceptional, but Mikey was phenomenal. Mickey's ability to integrate his speed with his ball skills again proved dazzling for the defense line.

Mr. Neville knew he had found a winning team; with Travis and Mikey's collaboration, they would be unstoppable. Travis, however, was euphoric about his performance. He surpassed his expectations. Travis impressed everyone and earned his permanent place on the team. He wore the number 10 shirt but still had eyes on Mikey's number 7. Travis knew he was skillful but not as impressive as Mikey and he envisaged being the best by whatever means necessary.

Travis was about to leave the field when he saw Woo across the sidelines. His eyes fixed steadily on her beauty as if it was his first time to see her. He wondered to himself if she had witnessed his brilliant performance. Other girls tried to seek Travis's attention, but he only had eyes for Woo.

Travis was about to walk over towards Woo just before seeing her kissing Mikey. Such action infuriated him, another reason to hate Mikey. Travis wanted to take his anger out on someone or something. He wondered why Woo would be interested in Mikey; she never seemed like that type of girl.

After Mikey went inside the locker room to change, Travis quickly capitalized on the opportunity to speak to Woo. "Really, you are with Mikey?" Travis asked. "Not that it is any of your business, but we were together before his fame," she claimed, staring him with anger straight in the eye. "So, you are telling me that it's serendipity that you're dating the captain of the football team. You might fool everyone else but not me. You act like you are so different, but you're just like all these other girls," Travis stated. He knew that statement was hurtful, but he could be careless.

Woo raised her hand swiftly, slapped him hard on his face, and walked away. "Do not speak to me again," she turned around to warn Travis. All were unexpected. Travis was jealous of Mikey; he could not even think straight to realize that he had hurt the one person he fancied and desired more than anything in his life.

Travis noticed Mikey singing in the locker room while putting his shoes away. "Good song," Travis mentioned.

Travis did not hear one word Mikey was mumbling. He just wanted to see where his headspace was off the field. "You think so?" Mikey asked politely, sounding super excited in his little voice. "I wrote it," Mikey declared, happy that someone found his song interesting as any young songwriter would.

"That is fire, bro. I need a copy right now!" Travis exaggerates. "No, I am a Christian. No one even knows I write this type of music, plus there isn't any studio around," Mikey responded. "Man, that has a buzz. I have a studio. Take my number. Let's record the song and keep it between us in the meantime," Travis implied. He could not help himself from sounding presumptuous, like always. "Sure," Mikey replied before exchanging phone numbers with Travis.

Travis learned everything he needed to know about Mikey. Mikey was a beast in the game. But off the field, he was spongy, and Travis knows how to take advantage of people's generosity. Travis saw why Woo would be fond of Mikey. Their spirits matched, and he intended to change that. To come between them, Travis had to convert one. Woo was inexorable, so it had to be Mikey, plus his spot on the field would be rewarding.

Chapter ten

Mikey's Time to Meet Elusive

"Do me this one last favor," Travis suggested to Elusive while chilling at the tire shop. "No, I'm not killing Mikey; we need him to win the championship this year," Elusive declared. Elusive didn't attend as many games as he would like based on the problems he faced with the law, but he had ways of keeping up-to-date with events. "Who said anything about killing him? Mikey can keep his life, but what he cannot keep is Woo, the captaincy, or my spot on the field," Travis announced.

"You know Mr. Richie?" Travis asked. "Mr. Richie with the studio? Yes, I know him," Elusive answered. "Well, I need you to steal the studio equipment as soon as possible," Travis requested. "Wait a minute, isn't he your uncle?" Elusive asked, looking extremely shocked at Travis's intention. "Yes, him you can kill if you're feeling trigger happy," Travis advised. He already had hatred for Uncle Richie after the incident at the resort in Montego Bay.

Travis wanted the studio equipment urgently because he knew it was just a short time before Mikey would call, eager to record. Travis knew that 99 percent of the time, kids like Mikey who have limited access to the environment and resources will go beyond measures to capitalize whenever an opportunity presents itself.

Mikey's mom and dad had partially locked him away from the world after losing one son to criminals, afraid of losing another. However, Travis had more than enough motivational and inspirational speeches for persuasion. It will not be hard to influence Mikey. After all, Travis had Elusive, the most wanted man on the Island running errands.

Three days had passed. Travis and Mikey were at Elusive's house, listening to a song they recorded. Travis convinced Elusive that keeping the studio at his house was the best idea. With Travis's brilliance, it took him only two days to learn about the complete installation of studio equipment, recording, mixing, and mastering music sounds.

"Listen, this song will be number one when it releases," Travis stated. Travis turned the volume up so they could hear the bass bumping through the walls. "These are some excellent speakers, R.I.P, Uncle Richie," said Travis, caught up in the moment and forgetting that Mikey was around.

Mikey said nothing, so Travis assumed that Mikey didn't hear him showing no remorse towards his uncle. "Turn up the volume!" Elusive shouted.

"How many songs do you have?" Travis asked. "Only one song," Mikey replied. "Well, we need to make an album of twenty songs," Travis stated, selecting a high amount to keep Mikey well occupied. "That will be difficult with school, football practice, and choir practice," Mikey replied. "Man, if I had this kind of gift, I wouldn't be running around kicking a football under the scorching sun. Music is your gift. You should not take it for granted, or maybe you are just afraid of your dad," Travis taunted.

"I saw you on the football field like a boy enjoying his hobby, but your passion in the studio reveals what you truly desire. Your pen came alive and your vocals destined for a lucrative venture." Travis pressed deeper into his persuasion. He would not give up that easily. Mikey's best option would be to pursue music as Travis proposed.

Travis's Plan B would have been to convince Elusive to kill Mikey. It would have been easy. An advantage is that he saw the stolen pieces of equipment at Elusive's house. "Okay, let's do it," Mikey said, giving in just like Travis expected.

Before the week had ended, Travis released the first song on social media without Mikey's approval. He got as many of his associates to like, comment, and share the song. Travis knew that Mikey would be furious at first, but not for long. Once the love started rolling in, Mikey would become accustomed and feel the need to maintain his relevance. This could cause him to diverge from football like Travis wanted.

Three weeks after the song had blown up, Travis noticed Mikey did not return his calls or show up at the studio; he wasn't even at football practice. "Travis, you will be in the starting lineup tomorrow. Don't be late," said coach Neville at training. "What about Mikey?" Travis asked. " Haven't you heard?" Mr. Neville questioned. "Mikey and his parents migrated because someone leaked a song Mikey recorded on his phone," Mr. Neville explained. "Poor guy, he just lost his brother to the streets almost a year ago. I thought he was over it, but that song clearly spoke about revenge," Mr. Neville added.

Travis showed no remorse about Mikey's disappearance. He could vanish off the face of the earth as far as Travis was concerned. Travis was only happy Mikey claimed he recorded the song using a phone and did not rat him out. "Well, that worked out even more spectacular than I thought," Travis uttered. With Mikey eventually out of the picture, Travis had gained his spot on the field. Now would be the time to settle in Woo's heart.

Chapter eleven

Travis Finally Won Woo Over

Since Mikey disappeared, Travis and Woo grew closer as each day passed. Travis gave Woo his shoulders to cry on, waiting patiently for the right time to make his move. Repeatedly, he showed his tactics of capitalizing on the state of vulnerability.

In Woo's case, Travis's intentions were pure from when he first saw her on the beach in Montego Bay. Just like the definition of her name, he finally wooed her into intimacy with his charm and benevolence. Travis visited Woo every day at her class, where they had lunch together. Ordinarily, she would feel uncomfortable having a boyfriend in a lower grade, but with Travis's popularity, it didn't matter. Besides, all the other girls were jealous of her. Woo and Travis's affections grew by the second, and they swore that they would be together forever.

"Why did you keep to yourself at the resort?" Travis asked. "I heard so much about you, which did not impress my mom," Woo replied. "Come on, it cannot be all bad," Travis mentioned. "Well, let me see. She mentioned you were too smart to continually make dumb decisions. I don't know, was that good or bad?" She asked. Woo enjoyed taunting Travis.

"Well, now that you got to know me for yourself, what do you think about what your mom had said?" Travis questioned. "Yeah, you are intelligent. I will give you that. As for the dumb decisions, you sell weed at the tire shop," Woo finally declared, she held that in her head for a while. He was in shock. The whole time, Travis thought that he had absolutely hid the weed business from Woo, but it turned out not to be so.

He had one question in his head; how long has she known, and why is she still dating him after knowing?

"You thought I wouldn't figure it out after seeing Elusive there every day? Better be careful with him, too. You don't need an angel to tell you that his company is not the best to keep," Woo mentioned. She was concerned about Travis's safety; she wondered if he was unaware or purposefully deviating good moralities because of his mom's decision to leave him in Jamaica.

"I realize you think the world owes you. I can assure you it doesn't owe you anything. Whatever you put in is what you get out. Do not think your choices won't eventually catch up with you," Woo scolded.

"Are you coming to my game tomorrow?" Travis asked, trying to avoid further conversation about his weed business and being in Elusive's company. Travis hated for anyone to give him life lessons. Though it came from the virtuous Woo, it was still irritating to his ears. "I wouldn't miss it for anything in the world," Woo answered. "We could definitely use Mikey in the final game though," Travis mentioned.

"Who do you think released that song?" Woo asked. The question has been on her mind for a while. Travis saw it coming. "Well, my best bet is Mikey's mom," Travis replied. "Why would you even say something like that? Mrs. Gloria would never!" Woo declared. "I can't believe you would even mention such a thing," she continued.

"No, for real, think about it. That would be the best reason to give her husband so they could leave the community,"

Travis declared. "Why would she want to leave so desperately?" Woo questioned. "Well, she found herself in a love triangle with Elusive," Travis claimed. Travis knew that he needed something substantial to seal his accusations.

Woo was confused and didn't know what to believe. Woo knew Mrs. Gloria was unhappy in her residency after her older son's death. Also, Woo thought it over that Travis would not tell such a drastic lie about the most wanted man on the Island. "Wow! That is crazy. Honestly, I could swear it was you," Woo stated.

 "Or maybe, I was hoping you went through all that trouble to be with me," she declared. Woo knew Travis was not innocent like he portrayed in her eyes. However she had no hate for his insolence, Woo secretly liked the notorious boy. She knew Travis wasn't the best choice, considering how her dad and mom ended. But she could not deny her true nature for too long, the bad boys sparks.

Travis's phone rang, and it was his mom. "Hi son, how are you?" She asked. "I'm doing wonderful, mom. Just getting ready for my game tomorrow," Travis replied. "Great, me too," said Marvina. "What do you mean?" Asked Travis. "I wouldn't miss any of your games while you were here in America. There is no way I would miss your last game. It doesn't matter where in the world it would be," Marvina explained.

Marvina would do whatever it takes to support her children in their interest. Even if it means leaving work early or going to work late, risking her job, the worst nightmare as a single mom. Travis being so entitled was unable to appreciate her sacrifices. "I'm at the airport trying to get past customs. It was supposed to be a surprise, but I am not getting my driver, so I need you to ask your dad to pick me up," Marvina requested.

The following day was the final of the football season with Travis's team called Eltham High and another team from the country called Knibb High. Being the final game of the season and Eltham High as the home team, the whole community was out for the match between the two most successful schools of the tournament.

There were a lot of changes to this event. They would have scheduled the game earlier in the day, but with this being a final in the heart of the community, they had to play after rush hours. A game like this would normally be played at a more popular venue called GC College however GC College was occupied with Track and Field events so the football game was diverted fifteen miles further away to another venue known as Spanish Town Prison Oval.

After the two teams walked onto the field, the anthem played while everyone stood up with their right hand across to the left side of their chest ready to sing their hearts out.

Travis stared into the crowd hoping to get a glimpse of the beautiful Woo, but could not pick her out with the plethora of red t-shirts. The stadium could be empty as far as Travis was concerned; all he wanted to see was Woo.

The game began with Eltham High kicking from left to right, wearing their full red home jersey, and Knibb High kicking from right to left in their famous purple and white. Travis was standing over the ball wearing the number 10 shirt alongside his teammate Kemar, who wore the number 9 shirt, nicknamed K9. Though Travis took over the captaincy, with the mystery yet to unravel, the number 7 t-shirt remained safely in the locker room, bearing Mikey.

The referee blew the whistle, and the game started with Travis passing the ball back to his defenders. Knibb players attacked the ball vigorously, knocking over Travis's teammates. knibb players intercepted the pass and scored the first goal less than 40 seconds into the game. It was the fastest goal ever scored in the competition's history. Knibb players were bigger, stronger, and faster. Their forwards were vicious in attack, showing a high competency. Off the ball, their defense displayed playful mischief and evil.

Indeed, both teams had the biggest rivalry in the competition's history. While Eltham High won at their two previous encounters, Knibb High came with a vengeance. By halftime, Eltham High was already two goals down. The opponents outmatched Travis's team.

The second half started with the teams switching sides. Eltham High kicked from right to left, and Knibb High left to right. By this time, Travis's teammates showed exhaustion after being knocked all over and bamboozled off the ball by their opposition.

The coaching staff looked despairing. Fans had already started walking out, looking distraught. Unexpectedly, there was a sudden burst of excitement in the crowd. The phenomenal one, Mikey number 7, shown on the big screen, was all the hope that the fans needed to come alive. After a quick substitution and Mikey regaining momentum, his dominance with the ball reinvigorated their fans, the coaching staff, and especially his teammates, showing how essential he was to the team.

Mikey would have been the chief striker upfront, but the coach wanted a fresh pair of legs in the midfield after realizing that was where they showed the most weakness. With Mikey in the Midfield supplying Travis with the ball who was more than capable of executing with either foot, they had an equal chance of winning the game. If both players played up to their standards, coming back from two goals down would bring a planned result.

Mikey's fresh legs wore knibb High players out 70 minutes into the game. Mikey proved to be too nifty to handle. They fouled Mikey on the outside edge of the 18 yards box, which resulted in him scoring the first goal for Eltham High from a free-kick with his powerful right foot.

In less than five minutes after the first goal, Mikey was inside the penalty area twisting and turning with the ball. His agility proved unstoppable, dismantling his opponent's defense line. It gave them only one option, which was to foul him again. Mikey scored three goals in the match. Eltham High team won. Mikey received the awards for best player of the match and the tournament. The fans elaborated it was two goals for Knibb High and three goals for Mikey, indicating that it was a one man's team.

The game finished, and Travis headed home. He thought of Woo and wondered why she was not at the field or picking up her phone. Travis asked her friend Simone, who he met at the bus stop. "Simone, have you seen Woo?"
"Woo was not feeling well, she stayed home. She did not want to distract you from focusing on the game, so she chose not to call either." Simone explained to Travis.

Travis made it a couple miles away from home; when he heard an ambulance and saw a lot of smoke rising in the air. A car pulled up suddenly at his feet, when the passenger door swung wide open abruptly. "Get in the car," Elusive told Travis. Of course, he did so, uncertain about what he was about to face.

"It is done! We will take over," Elusive said. Travis wasn't clear what Elusive meant, so he asked. "What do you mean?" With the look of venom on Elusive's face, Travis was shaking as he asked the question.

"After I finally told the gang what you had said to me about Gunhand, they were all in on the idea of me taking over. So, we waited until we knew Woo was gone to the game, then, we killed him and burned the entire house to the ground. That is all ashes now," Elusive bragged.

Travis rushed out of the car and ran breathlessly to Woo's house. He thought of their last conversation when she mentioned his choices catching up with him. To Travis, this would be the worst possible repercussions. Travis skipped through enormous crowds until he finally arrived at the spot, only to see.

To be
continued...

Moment of Thoughts
with the Characters

What were the thoughts running through your mind as you read through the lines of the book?

What are your expectations or predictions of the characters' future predicaments?

Do you share similar experiences with any or all the characters?

Share thoughts on the pages of each character while you read their stories in this book. Send them to my email at roshanejglewis@gmail.com

I appreciate you for reading, and I will love to read your views.

Thank you.

Marvina

Travis

....
....
....
....
....
....
....
....
....
....
....
....
....
....
....
....
....

I appreciate you for reading thus far and I will love to keep in touch with you, Dear reader.

Contact me via:

Website: www.roshanelewis.com

Email: roshanejglewis@gmail.com

Instagram: www.instagram.com/ishanemusik

YouTube: Ishanevevo

Thank you!

Other Books by the Author

Grab your copy;
www.amazon.com/dp/B09TDW94KX